Bee Paradise
Copyright © 2019 Written by Carolyn Clackdoyle
and Illustrated by Luminita Serbanescu.
Song: words and music by Carolyn Clackdoyle,
arranged by Krista Norman.

Tellwell Talent
www.tellwell.ca

ISBN
978-0-2288-0641-7 (Hardcover)
978-0-2288-0640-0 (Paperback)

A Bee Paradise grows in a garden, in a parking lot, near the Ottawa River. Look on the back cover of the book to see a map of Bee Paradise. Meet the raccoon family in the garden.

It's almost sunset. There is still time to visit the bees before it gets too dark. Mama Raccoon wakes up her raccoon kits by singing the Bee Paradise song. All of the young raccoon kits like to sing along…

Every evening, Mama teaches her kits about the bees. "When you are older, you will explore the whole city like a honeybee. Now, you are young. Just like the wild bees, you stay close to home."

Mama Raccoon loves wild bees so much that she gave her kits wild bee names: Bombus, Carder, Polyester, and Andrenid.

Kids, what sounds do you think raccoons make?
What sounds do bees make?

"Bombus, please lead us out the door. Carder, you're next," Mama chatters.

Bombus squeals, "I see the honeybees through the trees flying home after work. They look tired, but I am not tired at all!"

Carder chitters, "Where do bees carry the pollen and nectar?"

Mama answers by chattering, "Farmers know where the honeybees go. Do you know, Bombus?"

Bombus growls, "To steal honey, you must fight a honeybee's sharp sword. Honeybees stop strangers at the hive door."

"Please be humble," chirps Mama, "don't fuss, and make room on the branch for the rest of us."

"I never felt a bee sting. Maybe I never will," clicks Bombus.

"If bees stop singing," clicks Mama, "that will hurt much more than a bee sting."

"If I had wings, I would fly across the mighty Ottawa River and follow a honey-bee right now," Polyester chitters.

"Could we take a train across?" titters Carder, "or a ferry boat?"

"Or," Polyester whoops, "we could find bicycles to ride."

"I see twelve *little yellow taxis flying* across the Ottawa River," Andrenid trills.

"Maybe little yellow taxis fly to the moon and back," trills Polyester.

"No, not to the moon! To Moore farm across the Champlain Bridge," chirps Carder.

"Beekeepers know how to keep the little yellow taxis dancing and healthy," chirps Bombus.

Kids, do you take little yellow taxis to visit honeybees on a farm?

"A farmer helps a queen bee make her colony a home," Mama chirps. "A safe and healthy place is where baby bees transform. They grow from egg, to larvae, to pupae, to adult, to the outdoors to explore. The worker bees and the drone bees help the queen grow her colony."

"How many honeybees live together in a colony, Andrenid?" chirps Carder.

"More than five. More than five thousand!" Andrenid clicks, remembering, "I saw a spring honey bee swarm of thousands more than ten. If you think you're smarter than me, you can count them again!"

Mama chatters, "One *little yellow taxi* flew back across the river to the Ornamental Garden. It's by the Experimental Farm. There are flowering plants from all over the world to welcome the bees."

"The bees can land on a bee helicopter pad – the digitalis flower," chitters Polyester.

Kids, can you show how fast bee wings move? Can you land carefully like a helicopter?

"There are big and small bees in the garden, are they friends?" clicks Carder.

Mama clicks, "Museums can answer our questions. Maybe bigger honey bees and smaller wild bees can work together to help pollinate flowers so more fruits and vegetables can grow. We can ask a farmer who should know."

Bombus chirps, "In the great outdoor gardens, I feel well."

"The Iris might be in bloom," chirps Carder. "Can you tell?"

Bombus whoops, "Dance in a garden wherever you are! Honeybees dance in a circle if flowers are close. They dance in an 8 if flowers are far."

Kids, which honey bee dance will you dance?

Mama Raccoon chatters, "Our *little yellow taxi* is now at the Fletcher Garden by the Rideau Canal. I will take you there one day to see the wild flowers. Everyone loves a local diner where local foods are always on the menu."

Polyester trills, "There's a bee hotel in that garden and many B&B (Bed & Breakfast) homes for the small wild bees."

Bombus chirps, "Wild bumblebees live together in a nest. Maybe they live in a pile of compost, or in an animal hole in the ground."

"Maybe they live in a bird house someone lived in before, or maybe they sleep under a shed floor," chirps Polyester.

"Bumblebees might live in nests of five hundred or many more," trills Andrenid. "They are a big wild bee so they are easy for me to count and see. I think wild bees grow exponentially with the power of wildflowers."

"I am so very pleased that my kits know a lot about wild bee homes," chirps Mama.

"The *little yellow taxi* is back by our tree in the Bee Paradise," chatters Mama, "yippee-dee-bee!"

"I'm careful not to crush a bumblebee or wild flower because I'm gentle with my raccoon power," chirps Bombus.

"I am never a thief or a pest! I only eat what I need and I share the rest. What I like the most is that flowers will grow from food compost," chirps Polyester.

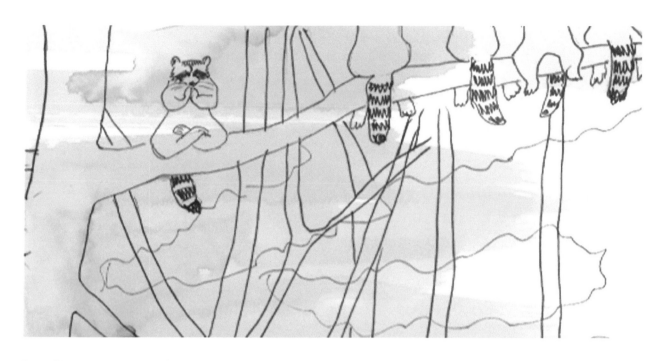

"Will we soon go down the tree?" whines Carder.

"We must wait for the car to go," Mama Raccoon growls that the car is still by the garden. Turning around for a different view, she relaxes and starts to purr, "Take a deep breath. Breathe slowly like the plants." It helps to feel the garden growing, clicks Mama to herself.

Kids, can you sit still and breathe
like raccoons in this tree?

Mama Raccoon thinks about her home, her kits, and her whole 'kitult' life. She is all grown up and a mama at two years old. Everyone is growing up and growing older in the garden.

Kitults and kidults are made-up words
that Mama Raccoon uses for grown-ups.

Kits and kids are real words that
Mama Raccoon uses for the young.

Do you know who helps plant the flower seeds?

Mama knows who plants the garden. "We live in a beautiful neighbourhood," she chatters. "From this tree, I can see the beauty around me. There is a pre-school, a building for seniors to live, a church, an apartment building, and trees all around the garden. A long time ago, there was just a parking lot. Now there is a Bee Paradise. The gardeners visit almost every day. Gardeners, just like plants, are old and young, big and small, short and tall."

"Can we follow the bees in Paradise before the sun sets today?" Whines Carder.

"Soon," chatters Mama, "when kids and kidults are in their beds."

"Kidults look at the flowers and tell stories and stuff. If we go down to the garden now, they won't bother us," chirps Bombus.

"I see over the lilac tree, into the windows with the lights," chirps Andrenid. "There are cozy rooms. The rooms look like bee burrows, just like little cocoons."

"The gardeners have left and their church door is locked. Will someone open the door when somebody knocks?" chirps Carder.

"A woodpecker knocked and made our den door. I think squirrels lived here before," chirps Andrenid.

"The car is wheeling away now, so can we go down and play?" whines Carder.

"Follow me," chatters Mama. "One, two, three, four; down we go to the garden floor."

"The time is right
    to go to the roots
of the maple tree!"

"You can look for something to eat, maybe a snail. You might find some rotten fruit from a tree on the garden trail," chatters Mama. "I like to wash my paws too."

"Let's make a shadow puppet," squeals Bombus.

"Ok," purrs Mama. "If you were a bee, would you look like you?

A head… yes you do.

Three eyes on the top to see light in the sky?

Many eyes on each side to see danger nearby?

A hard back that keeps you strong?

Two pairs of wings to fly?

A long tongue to drink nectar from a flower?

You might have a tail with stinging power.

Do you have two back legs with baskets to carry pollen? That's plenty!

Plus four more legs are not too many!

Antennae? How can you smell or fly if you don't have any?"

Mama chatters, "Keep your raccoon eyes sharp to find wild bees before dark."

Andrenid purrs, "I count Andrenid bees everywhere. I see burrow doors in sticks, in soil, and in rotting wood. It's ok that wild bees don't share honey with me. Wild bee honey is for bee babies."

Kids, do you like to eat honeybee honey?

"Some flies pretend to be a bee but they can't fool me," snorts Polyester.

Mama chatters, "Try walking in another animal's tracks. When you follow bees, you will see that they live together or alone. They live in different types of homes."

"On their dinner plate is flower food they ate," Mama purrs. "They love the colours violet, purple, and blue. Bees see differently than we do."

Polyester trills, "In burrows by fresh water, I see a Polyester bee that uses sap from a special tree. The sap in bee bellies makes weird plastic stuff to waterproof a burrow room. That's more than enough! Most fascinating is their special plastic biodegrading!"

Carder chirps, "The Carder bee brushes fuzz off special leaves. These fuzz pillows become so strong that burrows could last, maybe, a whole summer long."

Bombus squeals, "The Bombus bumblebee dances left and right. This is how I dance in the twilight. I protect nests and give bumblebees space to fly!"

Kids, will you bumble dance and bumble sing with Bombus?

"The trees and plants grow with the wind, soil, and rain in the right climate range; but it's starting to change. Many days are dryer, and many nights rain harder. More floods and more fires change bees and wild flowers," Mama Raccoon clicks.

"Will the wild native bees be ok tomorrow, after today?" clicks Carder. "Will they leave, or will they stay near our home?"

"Well, that depends on what we all do… about climate change too," Mama clicks and clicks and clicks.

She raises high on her back paws. An idea becomes clear, as clear as raccoon eyes in the dark.

"The changes we need will begin in the garden and in a playground close to home," purrs Mama.

"Now climb back to our den, up you go, up you go. Take your bugs and your berries to snack on. In a leaf you can wrap them up tight," Mama chirps.

"A Leaf Cutter bee makes leaf rooms in a tree house," chirps Polyester. "And did a Mason bee mine this hole in our tree?"

"Yes, that's right, and now it's late at night," chatters Mama.

"If I were a Cuckoo bee, I'd live in another bee's nest. Then I could try different foods and recipes. Someday, I want to travel to another country," chirps Polyester.

"I hope one day to say hello to a Sweat bee. Will it see me?" chirps Carder.

"Maybe not; you wear fur all year long," snorts Polyester.

"It's time to nap," chatters Mama. "After we nap, we'll explore the park again in the dark. My 'kits and caboodle,' it's time for a tune-up."

ACKNOWLEDGMENTS

We owe all our gratitude to local bee-friendly gardens and their knowledgeable gardeners. The Friends of the Meditation Garden at the First Unitarian Universalist congregation campus in Ottawa know how to grow paradise close to home! Their eco-system, lovingly cultivated for decades, is our Bee Paradise. The meditation garden peace pole was crafted by their minister reflecting a vision for all gardens. The word "church" in this book is used non-denominationally simply because it is a word that the raccoons "chirp."

We would like to thank our National Capital Region in Canada for preserving places that feed the bees and feed our curiosity

We searched for bees on the Internet. We found bee facts for our story with 'Friends of the Earth bees' and 'Christopher O'Toole bees' and 'David Suzuki bees'.

Lu and Caro have a poetry/painting/music collaboration and hopefully more Bee Paradise books. Visit www.codehoney.ca

Lightning Source UK Ltd.
Milton Keynes UK
UKHW052157190422
401760UK00002B/171